D0274648

First published in hardback in Great Britain by HarperCollins *Children's Books* in 2017

10 9 8 7 6 5 4 3 2 1

ISBN 978-0-00-8135089

HarperCollins *Children's Books* is a division of HarperCollins *Publishers* Ltd.

Text and illustrations copyright © David Mackintosh 2017

Designed and lettered by David Mackintosh   www.profuselyillustrated.com

The author/illustrator asserts the moral right to be identified as the author/illustrator of the work. A CIP catalogue record
for this title is available from the British Library. All rights reserved. No part of this publication may be reproduced, stored
in a retrieval system, or transmitted in any form or by any means, electronic, mechanical, photocopying, recording or
otherwise, without the prior permission of HarperCollins *Publishers* Ltd, 1 London Bridge Street, London SE1 9GF

Visit our website at: www.harpercollins.co.uk

Printed and bound in China.

For
beautiful
Minky

THERE'S A BUG ON MY ARM THAT WON'T LET GO

David Mackintosh

HarperCollins *Children's Books*

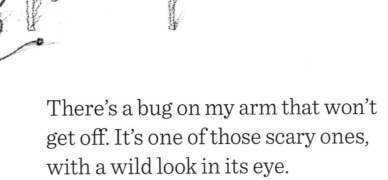

There's a bug on my arm that won't get off. It's one of those scary ones, with a wild look in its eye.

It could bite,

or WORSE...

IT COULD BE
A STINK BUG!

There's no way in the world
I'm going to touch it and I don't
want it anywhere near me.

O'Reilly's no help because
O'Reilly wouldn't hurt a fly.

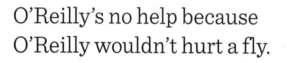

All Mum and Dad say is,

"Take it OUTSIDE."

But that bug doesn't want outside, it just wants ME.

Melody next door screams,

"IT MIGHT BE POISONOUS!"

and runs back inside. Her mother tells me
Melody is staying inside today.

And
Pearl
just sits
in the
sun.

NOBODY
wants
to know
about
that bug.
Not even
Melody.

So why
won't it
**BUZZ
OFF?!**

I remember the day Melody was sent home from school because the nurse found something in her hair.

Melody's mum said it was probably a flea from Pearl.

So Pearl had some cream squirted on her neck.

And Melody had to use a special comb and shampoo.

The next day, O'Reilly wasn't his usual self.

Mum said that it was probably a flea from Pearl. Or Melody, Dad said.

So O'Reilly had some cream squirted on his neck.

I still wonder where that flea went.

This bug needs my help – just like Melody when everyone called her Scratchy. I told them that Melody probably didn't want to have scratchy hair and *how would they like it?*

This bug needs to flap its wings, swim a few strokes, or find the right kind of leaf to sit on.

Instead,
it clings on
EVEN TIGHTER.

If it was me,
I'd prefer feeling soft fur
under my feet – not a
spongy arm.

Or long golden hair, like
Melody's. But she's not
coming outside today.

And Pearl
just sits there
in the sun.

When Melody's family moved in next door she was always snooping...

...like she wanted to see what we were up to.

Dad said that Melody might like to come over one day.

So I asked her, and she brought Pearl. And her own lunch.

Then Melody and Pearl and O'Reilly and me were friends.

Melody must be bored inside, all day, on her own.

Well, if I were that bug,
I'd like friends to play with.

And the shade of our big tree on a hot day.

Or the sun shining on
my back sometimes.

But that bug just sits there.

IT DOESN'T KNOW WHAT IT WANTS.

And when I think it can't be worse...

There's a BIRD on my head that won't get off. It's a heavy one, with scratching claws and a wild look in its eye.

I stand perfectly still.
Except for my knees
which wobble a bit.

I hope it's not one of those woodpeckers.

But that bird doesn't want ME at all.
It has something else on its mind...

MY

BUG!

So I take that poor
little bug out of
harm's way,

and that hungry bird buzzes off.

Thanks, Pearl!

My little bug is lucky Pearl is here to keep it safe.
And lucky I'm here, too.

When I see Melody tomorrow I'll tell her
about my bug, the bird, and Pearl.

In the night,
I hear
HISSING,
and
CLICKING,

and I wake up.

I think the bug is
saying something.

I listen closer,
and hard as I can.

But I can't make out
the tiny words, so
I whisper,

"What did you say?"

And that bug says at the
top of its tiny voice,

"Thank   you

Goodbye bug.

Look after yourself.